Jeff The Killer

By: Neesha Nickleson

CHAPTER 1

"Naomi, are you ready to go?" My mom called me
from downstairs. I grabbed my suitcase and pillow
and headed downstairs.

"Yes, I'm ready." I sighed. "Do I have to go to
camp?"

"Yes, you do. I signed you up and paid for
everything."

I went out the backdoor and put my things in the
trunk. I got in the front seat.

"You'll have fun Naomi." Mom said, "You might
even meet someone there."

"Sure mom; you always say that." I put my
headphones in. I always get this feeling when
something bad is about to happen. I got that feeling
on the way to camp and something usually always
does happen. Last time it happened, I cut my hand
open while slicing lemons and limes for juice. I still
have the scar. We got there and I got my stuff out of
the car and went to find out where my cabin was.
On the way there I passed a kid who looked like my
age. As I walked by him that feeling got stronger, but
I dismissed it. I stopped and looked at him. He had a
white hoodie on; he also had short brown hair. "Why
would you wear a hoodie during the summer?" I
thought. He looked at me. He had blue eyes I
couldn't help but stare into. He smiled at me so I

looked away and kept walking. I mumbled, "Weirdo."

I met my counselors and campmates and we went to our cabins. We had two hours before dinner. I put my stuff down by one of the beds and walked outside to the fire pit and plugged in my headphones. I sat there for a while and when I was changing my songs I heard a branch crack. I got up and then I took my headphones out and listened. It sounded like it was behind me, but I didn't want to look. I was afraid it was some kind of wild animal. I felt a hand on my shoulder. I screamed and turned around to see the kid from earlier. "Oh I'm sorry, did I scare you?" he asked.

"Yeah, kind of," I said.

"My name's Jeff."

"I'm Naomi."

"I noticed earlier you were staring at me; why?"

"Oh I was just…" I stopped and thought; why was I staring? So I made something up. "I was staring because you're wearing a hoodie during the summer."

"Yeah so?" he said.

"It's weird," I said.

"It's the way I dress," Jeff said.

"No not really." I sat down and Jeff sat next to me. "So have you made any friends here yet?" Jeff asked me.

"No, I'm not really the social type. What about you?"

"Uh, well no, but there is this blonde who has apparently developed a crush on me. Speaking of which, there she is."

A girl with blonde hair and green eyes walked past us. She had on a pink shirt, a pink skirt and pink flip-flops.

"I think this girl likes pink," I said.

She looked over and saw Jeff. "Hi my future husband, Jeffy!"

"Hi Mallory," Jeff said in an annoyed tone.

I turned and mouthed, "Jeffy, really?"

Jeff just shrugged his shoulders. She came over and sat in between us, pushing me off the bench.

"Hey!" I yelled.

"Oops, my bad; did I do that?" Mallory said sarcastically. I got up. "Are you ok?" Jeff asked.

"Yea I'm fine."

"Jeffy, don't pay attention to her. I'm so much better than that." She pointed at me when she said 'that.' I felt rage boiling inside me. I wanted to slap those blonde highlights out of her hair.

"Mallory, please don't do this," Jeff said. She didn't listen.

"She knows I'm better than her. I'm richer, smarter, more popular..." and she stood and got in my face... "And I'm much prettier!"

JEFF'S PERSPECTIVE

I knew that last comment pushed Naomi over the edge. I watched as her body tensed up. I knew she was going to do something she would regret.

"Did you really just say that?" she asked.

"Yea I did, what are *you* going to do about it?"

I heard the challenge in her voice. Then I saw it. Mallory had hidden a knife in her skirt pocket. I got up. I didn't know what to do, and then I got this weird feeling. I felt dizzy and dropped to my knees, my vision clouded. Mallory grabbed the knife and twirled it.

"You see, I can make you beautiful if you let me."

"No, get that thing away from me," I heard Naomi say.

"Oh come on, it won't hurt that bad." Mallory grabbed Naomi by her shirt."

"Let me go!" she screamed.

Then I blacked out to more screams. I woke up and Mallory and Naomi were gone. There was some blood on the ground. I got up. "These feelings keep getting worse and worse," I mumbled. I walked around and saw a cabin with pink light and heard a bunch of laughing girls.

"Now I'm sure that Jeff will want to be with me since that other girl won't be around him anymore." I got closer to the cabin when I heard Mallory's voice.

"So what did happen to Naomi?"

"Well, what happened, Jane, was that I was only going to make her beautiful like me of course, but sadly she refused and pulled a knife on me."

"So what did you do next Mallory?" another girl asked.

"Well Sally, I was quick and took the knife from her and cut her. See this is the knife I took from her."

"So did you kill her?" Sally asked.

"Of course not, I just merely scared her. I guess I don't need this knife anymore."

I heard the cabin window open and Mallory threw the knife out. I picked it up; it had blood on it. I touched the blade and an image flashed in my mind. I shook my head, freaked out by what I saw. I put the knife in my pocket. I figured I would need it again, but I just didn't know when. I walked around more to see if I could find Naomi, but I walked all around the camp and couldn't find her. The only place I hadn't looked yet was the lake. I walked down there but I couldn't find her. I started to get worried; what if Mallory had lied about killing her? I sat down in the sand.

"I don't know why I didn't stop her," I said.

"Stop who?" I heard someone say.

I looked around.

"Up here," the voice said.

I looked up and saw Naomi on one of the tree limbs that over looked the lake.

"What are you doing up there?" I asked.

"I don't know, just hanging I guess." She jumped down. "What are you doing here?" she asked.

"I was looking for you."

"Why?"

"Because, I was worried Mallory had done something really bad to you," I said.

"Well she did, just look!"

She showed me her arm and it was all bandaged up; so was her leg. "She also cut my back and my waist," she said.

"That girl needs to go to therapy or something," I said.

"She needs more than therapy," Naomi said. "I've known her my whole life."

"Well that must have been really hard for you." I remarked.

"Yeah, it's been like this ever since we were little. It wasn't so bad back then; all she did was pull my hair, which turned into biting. Then when we were about ten, she got a click of other girls together to push me around. Then at twelve, that's when the knives came in," she said.

"Wow that's awful."

"Yeah it is." We sat down in the sand and watched the water.

"Blondes are crazy," she said. "I want revenge but my mom always says revenge is never the answer."

"If you want I could talk to Mallory for you."

"Are you sure? You don't have to."

"Yeah, I'm sure."

"Thanks! I would hug you, but I would bring more pain to my wounds."

I thought, sure I would talk to her, but I had something else in mind. The image flashed but I didn't dismiss it; I embraced it.

"We should get back," I said.

"Yeah, it is getting kind of late." I stood up and helped Naomi up. On the way back Naomi surprised me with a question.

"So Jeff, do you like Mallory?"

"Huh?"

"I asked if you like Mallory."

I stopped walking. "Why would I like a psycho?"

"I was just asking."

She walked ahead of me and stopped. I looked around her and saw why she stopped. There was a girl walking toward us; I realized that it was Sally. I ran up beside Naomi. Sally stopped and looked at us for a second.

"I have a message from Mallory to Jeff."

I stepped forward, "What does she want?" I asked.

"She wants to talk to you by her cabin," Sally said.

"Fine I'll go see her." I rolled my eyes. "Just between us, I don't like her. She's mean; I secretly think she's a witch!"

Naomi laughed. "Mallory is more than a witch; she's a rattle snake in pink flip-flops!"

"I don't know why Mallory doesn't want you hanging around Jeff; ya'll are cute together," Sally giggled.

Naomi coughed. I didn't say anything. Sally walked over to Naomi. "I'm Sally. Sorry about what Mallory did to you. I'm just glad she didn't kill you."

"I'm Naomi, and yeah, I'm glad she didn't kill me either."

"I have to go now; Mallory is probably looking for me."

"Bye," Naomi said.

Sally walked away. I sighed; I really didn't want to go see Mallory. So many images flashed in my mind at that moment.

"Hey Jeff, are you ok? You look a little pale," Naomi asked.

"Yeah, I'm fine," I said. "I guess I better go see what Mallory wants."

I started walking away.

"Jeff, I uh…" She started to say something.

"What is it?"

"Um, never mind."

I shrugged my shoulders and walked on. I looked back and saw her running back to the lake.

NAOMI'S PERSPECTIVE

I couldn't bring myself to tell him; I don't know why but I just couldn't. I sat in the sand and pulled my phone out. I had a text from my mom.

It said, "Hi honey how's camp? I hope you're having fun. Have you met that someone yet?"

I laughed at that last part. I had but I didn't want to tell her I did. I stood up and started throwing rocks into the lake. I stood there while the clouds covered the moon which shrouded the shore in complete darkness. "I guess it's going to rain; I better get back." I said to myself. I walked slowly back to the main campsite. It started to sprinkle, and then it went into a downpour.

"Can this night get any worse?" I said. I kept walking at the same speed back to my cabin. I came in soaking wet.

"Hi Naomi, I haven't seen you all day. Where have you been?" Katie asked.

"I've been around," I said. I changed into drier clothes and put on a camouflage jacket.

"This storm is crazy," I said.

"Yeah, I wonder where the rest of our cabin is."

"Probably in the mess hall playing cards or something," I said. I laid down on the bed and read one of my books that I had brought.

"You're going to have to tell him sometime," Katie said.

"Tell who what now?" I asked looking at her.

"Tell Jeff you like him."

"Who said anything about me liking Jeff?"

"Sally came by and told me how she said you two were a cute couple and how you were shuffling nervously."

"I didn't shuffle; I coughed," I said.

"See you just admitted to it."

"Shoot!" I mumbled. Katie laughed. The cabin door opened and two other girls came in.

"Hey May and Lacy."

"Hey," May said.

"We brought you two back a desert from dinner," Lacy said.

My stomach growled and I sat up realizing I missed dinner.

"Here is some banana pudding for Katie."

"Awesome, I love banana pudding."

"And a large brownie with vanilla ice cream drowned in chocolate syrup for Naomi."

"Awesome! I couldn't possibly live without chocolate. Thanks Lacy."

"You're welcome."

I ate the whole thing in about two minutes. I sat there for a minute and then lay back down and continued to read. I tried to ignore that nagging feeling in the back of my head. It just kept coming back stronger. I plugged my headphones into my phone and turned on Katy Perry's *Dark Horse*. I listened and read ignoring the feeling. Whatever it was I didn't want to be involved.

Our counselor came in and tossed a napkin with something in it onto my bed. I sat up and looked into the napkin. Inside it were three buttered rolls with honey inside them and they were still warm.

"Thanks Kayla," I said.

"No problem, you must have been really hungry because I didn't see you at dinner."

"Oh I was in the nurses' cabin getting some wounds taking care of." I showed her my arm.

"Oh what happened?"

"I cut my arm on a rock," I lied.

"Oh I hope you feel better."

"Thanks." I went back to reading and listening to my music. *Everybody's Fool* came on by Evanescence. I thought, this describes Mallory so much. I started to get sleepy, and just in time too.

"Ok girls, it's about lights out time," Kayla said.

I put a mark in my book and snuggled into the covers. I fell asleep straight away. I had the worst nightmare ever. I was walking along camp in the early morning fog and there was a trail of blood. I followed it to the cabin that was three away from mine. It looked really familiar. I didn't want to walk into the cabin, but the trail of blood lead to the door so I walked up the steps and slowly opened the door. What I saw was a bunch of bloody bodies of girls I recognized. One body was Mallory's. I screamed so loud I could have woken up the dead, but I'm glad I didn't. I ran out of the cabin as fast as I could into the fog.

"Where is everybody?" I yelled. I ran down the hill and bumped into someone or something. I stopped; in front of me was Jeff in his white hoodie, but it was all bloody.

He turned and looked at me and said, "I talked to Mallory and her friends for you." He held up a knife; it was the knife Mallory used to cut me.

"Remember this? I used this to 'talk' to her." He laughed.

"Who are you and what did you do with Jeff?"

He grabbed my shoulders.

"I am Jeff, Naomi."

I screamed, "SOMEONE HELP ME!"

I woke up in the middle of the night sweating; did that really happen? Then I heard a scream.

Chapter 2

JEFF'S PERSPECTIVE

I was in Mallory's cabin. I had killed all her friends and now she needed to pay for what she had done to Naomi.

"Please Jeff, don't hurt me. I promise it won't happen again."

"It's too late to promise anything now," I said.

She backed up and hit the cabin wall; she looked around.

"If you're looking for something to use to get away it's not going to work."

I held the knife up. She looked up.

"Isn't that the knife I used to cut your friend open?" She covered her mouth.

I laughed maniacally, "Of course it is…now. I'm going to kill you with it!" I stabbed her in the chest and whispered in her ear, "Go to sleep."

I stood up and was about to walk out when I saw a light just outside the cabin. I dove under one of the beds. The cabin door slowly opened and a girl walked in and shined the light around the cabin. The light shined on the back wall where Mallory's body lay. Whoever was in the cabin walked over to

Mallory's body and screamed, "This can't be happening! "

It was Naomi. I held my breath hopping she wouldn't notice someone else was in here. She pointed the flashlight around the cabin. I looked around too. The light ended up on my knife. I froze. "Please don't see my knife," I thought.

She dropped the flashlight.

"I really hope you didn't do this Jeff."

I stopped, did she know I was in here or was she talking to herself?

"I'm going to have to ask him tomorrow I guess."

She ran out of the cabin and I climbed out from under the bed. I picked up my knife and walked outside. I looked down; I needed a shower and a change of clothes. I was covered in blood and what smelled to be lavender perfume. I walked through the forest to the bath house; I didn't need anybody seeing me all bloody. After my shower I went back to my cabin and fell asleep. I woke up in the morning to a pillow in my face.

"What in the world?" I sat up.

"Good morning Jeff," I heard Joshua say.

"Sometimes this boy can be too happy," I thought.

I got out of bed and pulled on a different hoodie. I went outside and walked around some. The memories of last night came creeping into my mind. I started laughing; I really don't know why, but I did. I ended up walking to the lake and walked along the shoreline. I heard someone singing and walked a little farther down the shoreline. I saw Naomi with her headphones in singing to one of her songs. I quietly went over and sat beside her. She stopped singing and listened to the music.

"You have a very nice voice," I said. She jumped a little.

"Thanks Jeff."

She didn't look too happy to see me and I was afraid I knew why. I smiled slightly.

"So… have you heard about what happened to Mallory and her cabin?"

"No what happened?"

"She and her whole cabin were murdered last night." I acted surprised.

"Who would do something like that?"

"Yeah, so the camp is having us leave early. They don't want anyone else dying."

I frowned and thought 'Didn't expect that one coming.'

"I need a ride home," I said. She looked at me and pulled her phone out.

"Hi mom, camp is having us leave early. I need you to pick me and a friend up; he doesn't have a ride back home. Yes ma'am he's a boy. No ma'am we aren't. Yes you will get all the details on the way home. Love you too, bye."

I laughed, "My mom isn't even that nosy."

"My mom isn't nosy, she is just very curious."

She looked at her phone and sighed. "I wonder what could have caused this to happen to them," she said.

"Well sometimes people like that deserve to die," I said.

She gave me a look that said, "What are you trying to say here?"

"I'm going to go and pack my things I guess," I said.

"Yeah, ok."

I left the lake area and went back to my cabin. When I got there everyone's things were outside the cabin.

I sighed, "Why did I do it?"

I walked in and stuffed things in my bag. After I was done with that I put my things outside the cabin door and decided to go back to the lake and see if Naomi was still there. As I walked I thought about confessing about what I had done, but then I thought, '"Do you really want to go to jail?" For some reason I answered my own question out loud. "No I don't want to go to jail." I got back to the lake and looked around. Naomi wasn't there.

"Weird." I walked down to where we were sitting earlier and sat down.

"That was fast." I heard someone say.

I looked around, and then up in a tree. Naomi was hanging upside down with her headphones in.

"Oh yeah, I just kind of stuffed everything in my bag."

"I see."

She dropped down from the tree.

"My mom should be here soon." She looked at her watch.

"I wonder if they will be serving lunch before we leave," I said.

"I don't think so; they want everyone out of the camp as soon as possible. Because of the killings, they are shutting this place down now." She sighed. "I had so many memories from when I was a kid and used to come here during the summer when my mom was a counselor here."

Man she looks really bummed out I thought. She took off her small backpack and opened it.

"Want a marshmallow?" She asked me.

"No thanks, I'm good; wait hang on, you carry marshmallows around in your bag?"

"No, it was just some camp snacks I brought along with me."

"Oh, ok."

Her phone rang playing *Kingdom Hearts*.

"Hello? Oh hey, are you here yet? Ok, we'll be right there." She hung up.

"Come on." I followed her and grabbed my stuff on the way to the car. She opened the trunk and dropped her stuff in. I put mine on top of hers. I climbed in the back seat with her.

"Mom, this is Jeff and Jeff, this is my mom." Naomi said.

"It's very nice to meet you, Jeff." Her mom said.

"It's very nice to meet you too."

We drove out of the camp and onto the road; from here to back where we live it's probably a two to three hour drive. I messed around with the knife in my pocket. I sat there thinking why in the world I would do such a thing.

"Hey you ok?" I looked over at Naomi; her face looked concerned.

"Huh, oh yeah, I'm fine. Why are you asking?"

"It's just that you had a very serious look on your face and then you looked sad."

"Oh I was just thinking of my little brother and his safety, and how he depends on me, and stuff like that."

"Ah ok, I get it."

Then there was that awkward silence again. I thought what I did was a self-defense for a friend…friend is an understatement.

Naomi's Perspective

 I wonder what's going on through his head right now - the times when you wish you had mind reading powers. I mentally slapped myself. What am I thinking right now? Right, why would someone want to murder a whole group of teenage girls? I looked over at Jeff. No, I couldn't have been him; he's too sweet to kill someone. Don't know why I would think that. I shook my head and looked out the window. I plugged my headphones in like I always do and fell asleep. I woke up in my house up in my room when I heard a window break; then all I heard was a scream.

"Mom, are you ok?" I called. No answer. I got worried so I went down to check what had happened. I checked the living room, the kitchen, the dining room, and my parent's room.

"I guess the only room I haven't looked in is the family room." I was reluctant about going in there so I went into the kitchen and grabbed the largest knife in the knife drawer, which was about 7 and a half inches long. I knew I wasn't going to have a good chance going against someone with a gun, but possibly someone with another knife just maybe, but the thing is I'm not so quick on my feet. I walked slowly into the room and heard someone singing what sounded like the song *Awoken* by Wooden Toaster and H8_Seed.

"I try my best to block out the screams but they're haunting me in my dreams," is what I heard.

I stood in the entrance way at the broken window in the room and then I saw him standing over my dad. I nearly dropped the knife when he turned around. I stared at the completely white face, black rimmed eyes, black hair, and blood stained white hoodie. He started speaking.

"Hello Naomi, I hope you don't mind me barging in and killing your family." He laughed.

I don't know why but his voice sounded strangely familiar I just couldn't place whose it was. I gripped the knife, I couldn't just stand there and not do anything. I had to avenge my parent's death. I stepped into the room and started walking toward him.

Half my brain was screaming, "WHAT ARE YOU DOING? YOU'RE GOING TO GET KILLED!" The other half was screaming, "YOU AREN'T AFRAID! AVENGE YOUR PARENTS AND KILL HIM FOR

HIS CRIME!" "Why are you doing this Jeff?" I stood a few feet away from the boy and looked him dead in the face.

"If you're wondering why I did this, it's because I thought it was about time for your parents to go to sleep." He pointed the knife at me. "And I thought it was about time for you to GO TO SLEEP!"

I took one step and felt something go into my chest. I dropped the knife and watched as crimson blood spilled on the carpet... my blood.

"You're too slow," the boy said in a taunting voice. I fell backwards and looked into his face and it was like the face switched. I saw a boy with brown hair and blue eyes looking down at me. I finally managed to speak.

"Jeff, why?"

"So you finally noticed did you. Too bad it's too late for you to do anything about it." Everything was becoming dark.

"Just go to sleep now." I felt a hand on my face it felt leathery somehow, and then I heard footsteps walking away. I jolted awake and patted my chest and sighed.

"Good, I'm still alive." I mumbled.

"You say something Naomi?" My mom asked.

"No, I was talking to myself as I usually do mom."

"Oh alright what do you and Jeff want for lunch?"

"I want Arby's if that's ok with you." I looked at Jeff.

"Oh yeah, that's fine with me," He said.

"Alright, Arby's it is." Mom said.

I sat there. Why in the wide world was Jeff (or at least I thought it was Jeff) in my dream, well nightmare? I banged my head against the car window.

"Ouch."

Jeff laughed.

"You laugh at people getting hurt too?"

"Huh, oh yeah, it's funny if I'm not the one getting hurt." He laughed more.

"I laugh at my mom all the time when she chokes." We both laughed. I looked over and looked at his hoodie and frowned.

"Hey what's that?" I asked.

"What's what?"

"That." I pointed to a red dark red spot on his hoodie.

"That, it's um, really red cool-aid."

I stared into his eyes and saw utter nervousness but I dismissed it; like I said, he's too sweet to do something so gruesome.

"Yeah whatever you say."

I looked out the window again. I don't know why I had this gut feeling that he's the one behind all of silence, looking at my phone and wondering why I've been having these awful dreams lately. I tossed my trash in the bag.

"I wonder if this whole killing thing will be on the news," Mom said. "It might; big things like killings and stuff always end up on the news." I said.

"What do you think, Jeff?" I asked.

"Uh yeah, I guess it could end up on the news," he said while fidgeting with his pocket hoodie.

I leaned in close to him and whispered, "You're acting really strange."

"How am I acting strange?" He whispered back.

"It's like you did something completely awful."

"I don't know, I've just been thinking what if the killer chose a different cabin than Mallory's and chose yours or something like that."

I froze in my seat. "I guess I never thought about that." I said. "I could have been killed."

"I'm glad you weren't. I couldn't live without my little baby," my mom said.

"Mom, I'm not a baby anymore! I'm sixteen years old," I said.

"I know honey. I just like to think of you as still my little girl."

I looked over at Jeff who was trying his best not to laugh. I sighed and put my face in my hands.

"How much longer till we get home?" I asked.

"Well according to the GPS I would say about thirty more minutes until we get to Jeff's house," My mom said.

"Ok."

"Hey, you have any paper and a pencil I could use?" Jeff asked me.

"Sure," I said and dug around my bag tearing out a piece of paper from my journal and handing it to him along with a pen. He took it and started writing stuff on it. I sat there and messed with a string on my jeans.

"Here." He handed the paper back to me. I looked at him confused. "Open it," he said while not looking at me. I opened it and read it. "Now we can stay in touch with each other," he said.

"Yeah, thanks." I pulled out my phone and put his number in. "Turn around and smile," I said and held my phone up in his face. He turned and gave me a big smile and I took a picture for his contact. I heard my mom snicker a little bit. I just rolled my eyes. We drove through a neighborhood.

"Hey, this place looks really close to our house." I said.

"That's because we are a neighborhood away from our house," Mom said.

"Oh, got it."

"So I guess we will see each other again," Jeff said.

"What school do you go to?" I asked him.

"I go to Winchester Academy."

"I go there too."

"Oh that's cool."

We talked for a little bit until my mom pulled into a drive way. Jeff got out of the car and my mom popped the trunk open so he could get out his stuff. I climbed out as well and walked him to his house. Jeff knocked on the front door and a boy about three years younger than me opened the door. He had blonde shaggy hair and green eyes.

"Hey Liu," Jeff said.

"Jeff, why are you home so early?" Liu asked confused.

"There was an accident at camp and they needed everyone back home as soon as possible." Liu looked at me.

"Who is this?" He pointed his thumb at me.

"She's a friend I met at camp."

"Liu, this is Naomi, Naomi this is my little brother, Liu."

"Hi," I said.

"Hey, are you Jeff's girlfriend?" Jeff flicked his brother on the forehead.

"No, she's not."

My mom honked her horn.

"I guess I better go; see you later Jeff. Bye Liu."

I ran to the car so Jeff couldn't see the redness in my face. I hopped in the front seat and my mom drove off.

"So anything going on you want to tell me?" My mom looked at me with that 'is he your boyfriend' look on her face.

"Nope, nothing I have to say." I put my headphones in and listened to music until we got home. When we got there I took out my stuff, went upstairs, unpacked and laid on my bed till dinner time.

"Dinner is ready honey." My mom called to me from the stairs. I rolled off my bed, headed downstairs, and sat at the table.

"What are we having?" I asked as my stomach growled loudly.

"We are having spaghetti and meatballs."

"Oh that's great." I fixed my plate and grabbed two pieces of garlic bread.

"So, how was camp?" My dad asked me.

"Oh, it was alright I guess."

"Did anything interesting happen there?"

"Yeah, a whole cabin of girls got murdered!" There was silence.

"Let me make sure I heard you correctly; you said a whole cabin of girls was murdered?"

"Yep, you heard correctly," I said and took another bite of my food.

"How could someone do something so ruthless and vile?"

I shrugged and finished. "Thanks for dinner mom." I got up washed my plate, grabbed my phone along with my headphones, went upstairs, closed my door, and read a book or two and drew some stuff.

"Tomorrow is Monday, which means school!" I screamed into my pillow and looked at my phone. I could text one of my friends, but they were all probably doing homework or something like that. Some of the girls were hanging out with their boyfriend's, blah, blah, blah." I sighed and played a game on my phone. I looked through my contacts and selected a random one. I looked at the name. Jeff.

Hey it's Naomi what's up? I waited and my phone played the text message tone.

Oh hey, nothing much just being bored out of my mind.

Haha, same here and I figured all my friends are busy so I didn't want to text them.

Phone beeps. *Well I'm a friend aren't I?*

I texted him back. *Well yeah, but you're, well, you're you.* I sent the message and a couple seconds later he answered back.

I am, but I'm your friend, correct?

'Yes you are my friend. I actually get along with you well, unlike some other people, aka Mallory.'

I sent the message and got an immediate reply.

'Oh go turn on the news channel right now!'

'Ok.'

I walked downstairs and sat on the couch and turned on the news.

"There has been a recent discovery of a cabin of girls found dead this morning at the camp known as Camp Ivy." I sat there intrigued by what I was hearing.

"Here we have Mallory's mother, a victim of this terrible crime. Tell us Mrs. Marsh, who do you think did this?"

"I don't know who would want to hurt my sweet angel darling Mallory."

I laughed. "Yea only you would say that." I listened on.

"We even had a beauty pageant to go to tomorrow and my sweet baby girl was going to win her seventieth trophy."

"Yes that's quite nice but who do you think is responsible for this terrible feat?"

"My sweet girl never had any enemies except for that one girl who lives next door to us."

"I feel sorry for whoever has to be that poor girl." There was a knock at the front door.

"Oh boy, I just had to open my mouth didn't I?" I walked and opened the front door to see a bunch of news cameras and flashing lights.

"See just look at her; that's the face of a murderer!" I heard Mallory's mom yell. I shielded my eyes from the flashing lights. A camera was pushed into my face.

"Tell us did you kill the beauty queen Mallory?" I kind of stood there for a second and then took the microphone.

"No I didn't kill anyone, yeah sure, I hated that girl's guts, but you should know she's not as *sweet* and *nice* as you all think." I rolled up my sleeves on my shirt and rolled my shirt up to my side.

"These cuts are proof that Mallory isn't the sweet and innocent girl you think she is, she nearly killed me with her pink sparkly knife!" The cameras turned to Mallory's mother.

"Is this true, did your daughter have a pink sparkly knife?" One of the reporters asked anxiously.

"She did yes but…" She was cut off.

"You heard it here folks, the beauty queen Mallory was really a monster in disguise."

"That doesn't mean anything! That girl there committed this crime of killing my daughter and her friends!"

Mrs. Marsh was dragged back to her home while the camera people left. I walked back into the house and slammed the front door shut. "Stupid reporters, this is why I don't watch the news."

I looked at my phone and saw about fifty people had messaged me. I skipped through all of them and went straight to Jeff's message.

'I never expected that to happen.'

I sent a message back. *'Yea some people are out of their mind crazy.'*

 My phone beeped. *'Yeah, I'm just glad you didn't say anything to make you look suspicious.'*

'Yeah same here.'

"Naomi, go take a bath and head for bed" my mom called from her room.

"Ok," I yelled back.

'I have to go I'll text you later or probably see you tomorrow at school.' I plugged my phone in and headed out of the room then I heard it beep.

"I might as well check one more message before I go to bed." I looked at my phone.

'Alright I also have something really important to tell you, if I see you that is.'

I put my phone down and walked upstairs to my room and started the bath. "I wonder what he needed to talk to me about." I finished up in the bathroom and headed for bed.

Chapter 3

Jeff's Perspective

"Hey Jeff, what are you thinking about?" A hand waved in front of my face.

"What? Oh it's nothing you should worry about Liu." He sat next to me on my bed.

"Do you like that girl that brought you home?" he asked me.

"Uh, I have no comment." He laughed.

"So does that mean yes you do, or no you don't."

"I guess it's a yes." He snorted.

"No Jeff, it's not I guess, it's a yes thing."

"What are you talking about Liu?"

"I'm telling you it's a definite yes, for you anyways, so yes, you do like her."

"Sometimes you don't make sense Liu." I said and ruffled his hair.

"Yeah, I know I don't make sense." He got up off my bed. "Well I'm going to go to bed now. Tomorrow is the first day of our new school." He walked away.

"Oh joy! I get to make new friends." I got ready for bed and as soon as my head hit the pillow I was fast asleep. I woke up the next morning with Liu yelling in my ear.

"JEFF, GET UP WE'RE GONNA BE LATE FOR SCHOOL IF YOU DON'T GET OUT OF BED!"

"Ugh Liu, quit yelling in my ear." I pushed him away and sat up and rubbed my eyes.

"Hurry up; I'll be waiting for you in the kitchen."

"Wait, you got me up just so you could have breakfast with me?" I asked, ready to pop him in the face.

"Well yeah, pretty much. I know you don't eat breakfast and all but still…" I threw a pillow at his face.

"Get out you idiot!" He laughed and left. I rolled off my bed pulled on a black shirt. I buttoned my black pants, tied my shoes up, and headed downstairs. Liu was sitting at the table eating toast. I looked at the clock.

"Come on, you can finish that on the way to the bus stop." I walked out of the house and headed to the bus stop at the end of the street. "Hey wait up!" Liu ran after me. I stopped and walked with him.

"I bet this could be the best day ever." Liu said.

"It could also be the worst day ever." I leaned on the bus stop pole. "Hey guys." I turned around to see Naomi standing there holding a skateboard.

"Hello there." Liu said. She had her headphones in as usual.

"Hey. You ride a skateboard?" I asked.

"Yeah, not a lot, but I do when I come to the bus stop," Naomi said.

"You hear that?" Liu asked.

"Do we hear what?" Naomi asked and took her headphones out. I listened closely and it sounded like skateboards. Liu stood beside me. Three guys jumped over the fence on skateboards. One of them was as skinny as a twig, one was huge, and the other was just normal size and had on a hat. The guys got off their skateboards.

"Looks like we've got some fresh meat," the normal kid said.

"Oh great, it's you," Naomi said.

"Back off girlie, let me introduce my friends here to yours," the kid in the hat said.

"I'm Randy. That's Troy." Randy pointed to the fat kid. "And he's Keith." He pointed to the skinny kid.

"There's a little bus fee for new kids around here, if you know what I mean. So you can give us your money willingly, or we can beat it out of you," Keith said.

Liu stepped up and prepared to punch Randy, but I held him back. "Don't even think about it you dummy," I whispered to him.

"It looks like we'll have to do this the hard way," Randy said. Keith and Troy pulled knives out.

'Oh joy this again,' I thought. I dropped my bag on the ground and prepared to fight them off.

"Jeff, don't do something stupid," Naomi said. I nodded and got that strange feeling again as Troy came at me with the knife. I kicked him in the gut hard and he fell, dropping his knife. Keith came at me. I rolled out of the way and picked up the knife

Troy had dropped and stabbed him in the arms and legs. He screamed and went down hard.

"Looks like I'll have to take care of you myself," Randy said.

I dropped the knife and he came at me with a punch. I grabbed his arm and flipped him over, and then I punched him in the face. I wiped the sweat away from my face and picked up my bag.

"This isn't good guys, the bus is coming and if they see them," Naomi pointed to the guys on the ground, "we'll be in gigantic trouble. You two better run!" She jumped on her board and took off toward her house.

"Let's go Liu." I grabbed my bag and ran off toward the house.

"Jeff, wait!" Liu ran after me.

The bus pulled up right after we ran off.

"Man I hope the bus driver didn't see our faces." I ran inside the house and pulled Liu inside.

"Jeff, what you did back there was awesome!" He poked my cheek.

"I bet Naomi was really impressed," Liu said and sat on the couch and turned the TV on. I didn't say anything.

"So what are we going to do? We can't go to school because we'll get caught."

"I guess we are staying here for the day then," I said. There was a knock at the door.

"Oh no, is it the police?" Liu said and dove under the couch. I looked outside and opened the door.

"It's ok Liu." Naomi ran in the house.

"Shut the door; shut it right now and lock everything!" She jumped over the couch and hid. "Hey, it's nice to see you too," I said and locked the front door. "What's going on?" Liu asked and slid out from under the couch.

"Randy knows where I live! I barely escaped without him killing me," she said.

"Wait I'm confused, so your saying you ran all the way here just to escape Randy and his goons?" I asked perplexed.

"Uh yeah, where else was I supposed to go?"

"Good question," I said.

"Oh I also got cut too. The only thing we had lying around was a metal bat so I used that and knocked them all out, but then Randy cut open my arm."

I looked and saw a trail of blood on the tile floor to where she was standing.

"Jeez, don't just stand there and bleed to death; come with me." I grabbed her arm and led her into the kitchen while Liu followed closely behind.

"Liu, clean up the blood while I sew up her wound," I said while rummaging through the cabinets to find a needle and some peroxide.

"Ok." Liu got one of the sponges from under the sink and started cleaning the blood trail.

"How are you not crying right now?" I asked and moved her sleeve. "Who said I'd be crying; not all girls cry when they get hurt," she sighed. "It makes us look weak."

"Yeah, I get it. This might hurt a little." I cleaned the cut with a rag and the peroxide doing my best not to put too much pressure. She didn't even make a sound.

"Do you know how to sew a cut up?" she asked me.

"This may sound stupid, but my mom had me take a sewing class and I figured it's just like sewing, right?"

She looked at me a little scared. "Yeah, whatever, just hurry up!"

I sewed up the cut and cut the rest of the line off. "There we go."

"Thanks Jeff." She hopped down from the table and walked into the living room and stood there for a second. I scratched my head.

'Is this really the good time to do this now when all of this is happening?' I thought. Liu looked at me from over the couch. He was motioning with his head to something. I just shrugged and sat next to him on the couch.

"Jeff," he whispered in my ear.

"What?" I asked.

"I read your phone messages."

I blushed a little.

"Ok, I don't care."

"I know you were supposed to tell her something really important," he said.

I ignored him and looked at the clock. It was twelve o'clock.

"Is anyone else hungry? I'm about to die if I don't eat soon."

Liu frowned and elbowed me in the ribs.

"I am, but I don't want to stay here any longer than I have to," Naomi said and got up. Liu jumped over the couch and looked out the window.

"I wouldn't go out there if I were you. Randy and his goon troop are still outside."

"Ok, I guess I'm staying then," she said and leaned over the couch.

"Ok so what do we want for lunch?" I asked.

"Oh!" Liu waved his hands in the air.

"Yes Liu?" I looked at him.

"We haven't had pizza in a long time; let's have that." He smiled.

"Are you ok with that?" I looked over at Naomi; she still had her back turned to me.

"Yeah, that's fine as long as it's from Papa Johns."

"Ok, what kind do you want?"

"I'm good with either cheese or pepperoni."

I got up and went to the phone book, called the pizza place and ordered a large pizza and breadsticks.

"Oh, I just thought of something. Jeff we don't have money to pay," Liu said and flopped on the couch.

"Oh, you're right," I said.

"Don't worry about it, I always have money handy. I always beg my mom for spare change and dollars." She pulled out a wallet and dumped about fifty bucks and a handful of quarters out onto the table.

"Wow, that's a lot of money," Liu said.

"What did you do rob a bank or something?"

She laughed. "I'm not that skilled of a person, but I do pick pocket stuff," she said and held up my wallet.

"Hey give that back Nao," I said and reached for my wallet.

She giggled. "Nao? Is that my nickname now?" she asked and handed me my wallet back.

I blushed a little. "Uh oh yeah, you like it?" I asked.

"Yeah, it's great!" She smiled.

We sat on the couch and watched TV for a while until the pizza came. There was a knock on the door.

"I'll get it." Liu said and hopped off the couch and opened the door. "Here is your pizza and breadsticks," the woman said. Liu grabbed the box.

"How much money is it?" I asked.

"Twenty thirty-three," she said.

I grabbed the money off the table and handed it to the lady.

"Thank you."

She walked back to the car and I shut the door. Liu set the pizza box on the table, grabbed a plate from the kitchen, took his pizza and went upstairs.

"Well I'm going to watch TV in my room now."

I looked up at him and he turned his head and gave me a smug look. I glared at him. I looked over at Naomi who had already gotten to the pizza and was eating and listening to music. I grabbed a slice and ate it and thought, *'I have and idiot for a brother sometimes.'*

"Do you want my mom to pay you back for the pizza?" I looked at Naomi.

"Nah, you don't need to," she said.

I looked at what the TV was playing at the moment.

The screen was showing the opening for *Ben 10 Omniverse.*

"Want me to change the channel?" I asked.

"No you don't have to. I watch this show anyway," she said.

"I actually do too," I said. We sat there for a second and watched the show.

"Hey, where did Liu go?" she asked.

"He went up to his room with his food about twenty minutes ago."

"Oh I didn't notice," she said. I shuffled my legs nervously.

"Oh hey, you told me last night you had something really important to tell me," she said and turned to me.

"I did?" I saw something move out of the corner of my eye and looked up to see Liu sitting on the top step.

"Uh yeah, you did. See?" She showed me her phone.

"Oh I guess I did." I laughed nervously.

Liu snickered quietly.

"Come with me." I got up and walked to the stairs. Liu got up and ran to his room.

"Alright I guess." She got up and followed. I walked to my room.

"Don't mind the mess," I said shoving a pair of shoes under my bed.

"Hey, my room is messier than yours so I don't care." I heard loud music coming from Liu's room.

"Your brother is going to go deaf if he doesn't turn that music down." She laughed.

I walked over to Liu's room and banged on the door really loudly. "HEY LIU! OPEN UP!" I yelled.

Liu opened the door.

"Can I help you?" he asked with a smile on his face.

"Yeah, you can turn your music down please."

He shrugged and pressed the off button on his remote.

"So how's it going, Jeffery?" He raised his eyebrows at me.

"I was going to do it until you obnoxiously blasted your music." I flicked him in the forehead.

"Oops, I'm sorry about that." He laughed and shut his door.

I walked back to my room to hear singing. I stood in my doorway and listened to Naomi sing. I walked and sat in front of her; she had her eyes closed. She opened her eyes and fell backwards.

"Wow uh, how long have you been sitting there?" She looked really surprised.

"I've been here through half the song," I said and smiled. "You have a great voice."

She avoided my eyes. "No I don't; your just saying that."

"No I'm being serious." I stood up and held my hand out to her. She took it and I helped her up. I saw Liu peeking around the corner of my door.

"You remember how I told you that this thing was really important?"

She nodded.

"What is it?" she asked.

I looked away.

"Could you close your eyes for me?" I asked.

"Sure I guess." She closed her eyes.

I sighed and mouthed to Liu. *'Are you happy now?'* He nodded and grabbed his phone. I shook my head. *'Don't do it.'* He sighed and put his phone away and waved his hand at me.

I sighed. *'I have to do it sometime today.'* I thought. I leaned my head in and kissed her on the lips. I stepped back.

"You can open your eyes now."

She opened her eyes.

"Yes." Liu said, and then covered his mouth.

"Is that what was so important?" she asked and crossed her arms.

"Yeah, I like you, ok?"

I turned around. She blew hair out of her face. It was silent for a moment. I turned back around and she kissed me back. I nearly fell over.

"I like you too." She grabbed my arm before I completely fell over.

"You ok?" she asked.

"Yeah, I'm just a little surprised." There was a sound like a phone ringing going off.

"Oh, that's mine." She bolted out of the room and down the stairs. I walked out of the room and looked at Liu.

"See, that wasn't so bad Jeff." I hit him on the head, not hard but hard enough.

"What was that for?" he asked while rubbing his head.

"Liu, you're an idiot sometimes you know that?"

"Hey, I was just trying to help you." He frowned. I walked off downstairs.

"Yeah, I'm fine Mom! Ok, bye." I heard her hang up the phone.

"Is everything ok?"

"Yeah, my mom was just worried why I wasn't home and why the metal bat was covered in blood."

"Oh." I nodded.

"I just explained everything." She looked at her phone. "I'll be right back. I have to run something over to my house." She picked up her bag and walked out the house.

"Want me to come with you?" I asked.

"Sure, if you want to."

"I'll be right back Liu!" I yelled upstairs. I shut the door and walked beside Naomi.

"Hey there guys."

I stopped and turned around to come face to face with Randy.

"What do you want bonehead?" Naomi asked and got in his face.

"Hey, back it up girlie." He pushed her. She dropped her bag.

"Oh so we're fighting back again huh?"

"Push me again and see what happens."

He pushed her harder this time into a light pole. I watched, too shocked to do anything.

"Oh, you asked for it now." She walked up to him and punched him in the face. I heard what to me sounded like bones breaking. I cringed.

'Glad this isn't going the other way around.' I thought.
Randy hit the ground and he whistled loudly. Keith
and Troy came behind him.

"You don't have your little bat to back you up this
time little girl," Troy said.

She looked ready to murder all three of them with
just her bare hands. I grabbed her bag and took her
arm.

"Let's go. You can't do anything against all three of
them." I ran off and she ran behind me.

"Go get them both!" Randy said.

I looked back.

"Jeez, for a tub of lard, that kid Troy can run fast." I
ran faster. "I'll follow you since I have no idea where
you live."

"Ok got it." We ran down the street and past four or
five houses and ran up the driveway of big white
one. She unlocked the door and ran inside. As soon
as I stepped inside she slammed the door shut.

Chapter 4

Naomi's Perspective

"DAD, GET YOUR GUN!" I yelled.

My mom came running in. "Naomi, what in the world is going on?"

"Bullies were chasing us so I'd thought I'd teach them a lesson and have Dad run them off with his gun."

"Your dad isn't here right now he's on a trip." I crossed my arms.

"Well shoot. Wait I know." I ran and got my BB gun from the back door, pumped it a few times for extra power and walked back to the front.

"Oh no! You aren't going to shoot them are you? You'll go to jail," my mom said.

"It's not like I'm going to shoot them - I'm going to shoot at them."

I opened the door. Keith and Troy were in the driveway. Jeff stood next to me.

"Are you seriously going to do this?" he asked.

I nodded. "Yep I am. HEY YOU BONEHEADS, LOOK THIS WAY!" I yelled and pointed the gun towards them and shot it. Keith yelped and ran off Troy just stood there, then he screamed and ran off.

"So long suckers." I placed the gun over my shoulder.

"You are the most boyish girl I have ever seen in my life," Jeff said.

"Um, is that a bad thing?" I asked and walked inside.

"Not in your case," he said and followed me in.

"You two are adorable," my mom said.

"Mom, please don't do this."

"Oh, I'm sorry. I'll be in the family room watching TV if you need me." She left.

"I want to meet your parents if they're home now," I said.

"Yeah, they probably might be home by now," Jeff said. I walked into the family room. "I'm going back over to Jeff's house to meet his parents," I told my mom.

"Ok have fun."

I walked to the front and headed out the door. Jeff followed me. We heard sirens and saw a cop car drive by, lights flashing.

"I wonder where they're headed in such a hurry," Jeff said. I shrugged and rounded a corner.

"I think I just figured out where they are going." Jeff looked over my shoulder.

"You can't be serious," he said and looked at me, and then he ran off.

"H-hey, wait up!" I called and ran after him. We ran up the drive to his house.

"Jeffery, what is the meaning of this?" His mom was standing there in the doorway with a police officer.

"What are you talking about mom?" Jeff asked.

"I'm talking about what happened today at the bus stop." She had this stern look on her face. I knew I should have stayed quiet.

"There were these kids that were picking on me and Liu so I stopped them," he said.

"It's not Jeff's fault Mom." I heard someone say. I looked in the house and saw Liu standing there with a knife. The police officer pulled her gun.

"Drop the knife son and come over here," she said.

"I'm the one that hurt those bullies," Liu said.

"Liu no, that's not what happened at all! Please don't defend me," Jeff said.

"Liu, Jeff is right; you don't have to do this," I said.

"It's fine you two. I know what I did and I have to pay for it." Liu smiled a bit.

Liu walked over to the police woman and she hand cuffed him.

"Liu, please don't." Jeff looked distraught.

"Hey, keep my brother safe and out of trouble, alright Nao?" Liu said to me. I only nodded.

The woman put Liu in the back of the car and drove off.

"Jeff, come inside," His mom said. She looked at me. "You can come in to if you want, sweetie."

I nodded.

"Jeff?" I took his hand and he looked at me and we walked inside. We sat down on the couch. I sat there and listened to his tears drop on the couch. I reached my arm around him.

"I don't know w-why he didn't l-listen to m-me," he said through his tears.

"Jeff honey, you don't have to cover for your brother anymore," his mom said.

"I'M NOT COVERING FOR HIM! I'M THE ONE THAT BEAT UP THOSE KIDS IT WAS ME!" Jeff yelled and ran upstairs.

His mom sighed. "I'm so sorry you have to see him like this dear." She gave me a faint smile.

"I-its ok, I'm used to seeing people sad," I said and got up. "I'm Naomi." I extended my hand to the woman.

"I'm Mrs. Woods." She took my hand and shook it. "Could you go comfort Jeff for me? I want him to be happy for the birthday party for Billy tomorrow." She walked away. I walked upstairs and knocked on his door.

"Jeff?"

"GO AWAY!" I heard through the door.

"Jeff, open up or I'll kick down the door and you should know very well that I can do it to!" I shot back.

I heard a click and the door opened slightly.

"May I enter your room?" He opened the door more and I slid in.

"I know I shouldn't ask if you are ok because I know you aren't, so I won't ask." I sat on his bed next to him and put my head on his shoulder.

"You'll see him again you know. Kids don't stay in juvenile detention forever; he'll be out in a day or two," I said.

"Yeah, I know. Liu shouldn't be in there though, it should be Randy and his good for nothing idiots," he said.

"Yeah, I'm sorry I couldn't help you more on that situation. I should have backed you up more. If I had just said a couple more words and given them evidence of some kind, Liu would still be here." I looked at my trembling hands.

Jeff's Perspective

"It's my fault. I should have told you about the thug trio before we even started school. I'm so sorry Jeff." She got up and ran out of my room.

"N-no wait Nao, it's not your fault." I got up and jumped the stairs and bolted outside.

"Jeez she's fast." I ran after her and finally caught her arm. "Listen to me it's not your fault, I shouldn't have beaten them up in the first place."

Her whole body was shaking. "I k-know but still, if I h-had just t-told you about t-them he would still be here." She faced me. She wasn't crying as her voice sounded, she was just shaking incredibly hard.

"Look at me in the eyes." She looked up and I looked into her dark eyes; I could barely see myself in them. "Its fine; you didn't cause this. It's mainly my fault." I wrapped my arms around her and hugged her. "Are you alright now?"

She hugged me back. "I guess I'll be fine." I looked in her eyes again. She kissed me and I kissed her back. I broke off.

"I have to go back home now, my mom wants me rested for this kid's party tomorrow." I said.

"You're going to that too?" Naomi asked.

"Yeah, when we moved here the day before camp the kid's mom came over and asked if we could come," I said.

"The little guy thinks I'm his sister or something because I always babysit for them," she said and turned.

"Well, see you tomorrow."

She walked away and I watched her go; the street lights flickered on as she went. I walked back to the house, went inside, headed upstairs and took a shower.

"I really don't want to go to this party; I'm not really a fan of kids." I finished showering and dried off, put clothes on and lounged in bed and read.

"Jeff, turn out the lights; you want to be rested for tomorrow," my mom said.

"Ok mom."

She shut my door and I turned off my light and fell asleep.

Chapter 5

Naomi's Perspective

I sat in the bathtub and messed with some bubbles and sang *Welcome to the Show*, a song from the movie *Equestria Girls Rainbow Rocks*. I had my phone plugged up to my speaker and I was in my relaxation mode. I sang along with all the songs that came on until it came to one specific one called, *Fallen Angel*. I dunked my head under the water. I listened to the music; I could faintly hear it. I couldn't help but imagine while I was under there.

I stood in a large ball room in a red flowing dress that came to my knees. I walked around, my footsteps echoing throughout the hall. I felt a hand on my shoulder and I turned around to see Jeff in a suit. "Would you like to dance with me?" he asked and smiled. I took his hand.

"I'm not a good dancer, just so you know."

"I bet your dancing is as good as your singing." He put his hands on my waist and I put mine on his shoulders. It was amazing! I had no idea I could dance that well and the music made it even better. Just as we were about to kiss, I felt a tap on my head, lost my breath, and my imagination flooded away. I popped up to see my mom.

"It's time to get into to bed," she said.

"Ok." I pulled the plug, got out, got dressed and jumped into bed. Mom took my phone down with her.

"Goodnight, I'll come wake you up before we have to leave."

"Ok." I closed my eyes and fell asleep. The next morning my mom came upstairs and put a box on the ground.

"Wake up it's almost time to go."

I snorted and sat up.

"Do I have to go?"

"Yes, Billy loves you; he would be so sad if you didn't come."

I got up.

"What's in the box?" I asked and opened it.

"I bought it for you to wear to the party." I pulled out a red dress and gasped. "Thanks mom," I said. I put on the dress with my black boots and headed downstairs.

"Ready?" my mom asked.

"Yep, as ready as I'll ever be."

I walked out and down the street three houses to a gray bricked house with balloons. I walked into the back yard and saw a ton of little kids, ages five to about eight. I stood next to the fence. A little red head boy came running up to me and jumped into my arms.

"Hi, Naomi! I'm so glad you made it to my birthday," he said.

"I wouldn't miss it for the world kiddo." I hugged him and set him down and he ran off.

"Who was that?" I heard someone ask. I turned and saw Jeff walking in.

"That was Billy." Jeff was dressed in his white hoodie and black dress pants. I giggled.

"What's so funny?" he asked.

"Oh, what you're wearing, it's your usual hoodie and black dress pants. The pants are completely different from the hoodie."

"I didn't want to wear anything fancy," he said.

"My mom bought me this dress for the occasion," I said.

"It looks good on you," Jeff said.

I looked at the fence on the other side of the yard and saw something moving behind it.

"They're back again," I said.

"Who is?" Jeff looked at me.

I whistled loudly.

"BILLY, GET YOUR FRIENDS IN THE HOUSE NOW!"

Billy ran in the house with everyone else. Randy and his duo of friends jumped the fence.

"It's payback time." Randy said.

Jeff's Perspective

"You again, how many times do we have to beat you up?" Naomi said.

"Stay out of this," Keith said.

"We don't want nothing to do with you girlie," Troy spat.

"We're here for your little boyfriend," Randy said.

"If you want me come and get me," I said.

"I want to help!" she said.

"No, I'm not risking you getting hurt again."

She growled. "Fine, but if you need me I'll back you up."

Randy came at me first and tackled me through the glass door, shattering it. He punched me in the jaw and threw me off of him. I staggered back and fell. I looked over and saw Keith and Troy with guns preventing the grown-ups from helping. I picked a piece of glass off the ground. It cut into my hand but I didn't care.

I got that feeling again, but this time it didn't want to go away. I threw my body at Randy knocking him over and slitting his throat with the glass, stabbing him repeatedly. I stood up. Randy cracked a bottle of vodka over my head before he fell. The liquid dripped over my body. Keith dropped the gun.

"You're in so much trouble now boy!"

I ran up the stairs and into the bathroom. Keith tackled me into the shower curtain and it fell. I grabbed the rod and hit him over the head. I stepped out of the shower and he punched me. I hit the medicine cabinet and a bottle of bleach fell over and opened on top of me. It burned a little but I still didn't care. Keith laughed.

"What's so funny?" I growled.

"Your face is covered in bleach and vodka." He laughed and threw a lighter in my face lighting my whole body on fire. This time it really did hurt. I screamed in agony.

"JEFF!"

I looked over to see Naomi in the doorway, then I blacked out. I woke up to hear the beeping of a heart monitor.

"I can't see anything!" I said to no one in particular.

"Oh good, your awake," I heard a woman's voice say. "The reason you can't see is because you have bandages over your face," she said.

"Where am I?" I asked.

"You are in the hospital; you suffered severe burns," she said.

"When will I get my bandages off?" I asked and tried to sit up.

"You'll get them off soon, and please try to rest, okay?"

She left. I laid back down and fell asleep. About an hour later I heard the door open and woke up slightly.

"Good news, the doctor told me you'll get your bandages off in an hour or two!" the nurse said and then she left.

I flopped on my pillow. "How am I even still alive?"
I heard the door creak open.
"Jeff?" I heard a girl's voice.
"Yeah, who is it?" I asked and sat straight up.
"Who do you want it to be?" she asked me.
"I would love to see Liu, my mom, and my amazing
girlfriend," I said.
"You're request has been granted," the girl said.
"Is this Jeff's room?" I heard a boy's voice.
"Liu is that you?" I asked hopefully.
"Yea it's me." Liu said.
I smiled through my bandages. "Wait is mom here?"
I asked.
"Yes, I'm right here honey," my mom said. I felt
someone sit on the bed.
"No need to ask about your amazing girlfriend
because I'm here."
*I'm glad I have these bandages on I don't want her to see
me blushing,* I thought.
"So how long have I been out?" I asked.
"About three days," Liu said.
"THREE DAYS!" I yelled.
"Yes, that's what I said," Liu said.
The door opened.
"Alright Jeff, it's time for those bandages to come
off," the nurse said. I felt a hand on mine and I got off
the bed and was led in front of a mirror.
"May I take the bandages off myself?" I asked.
"Sure you can," the nurse said.
I reached my hands up and untied the bandages
around my face. The bandages unraveled and fell at

my feet. I blinked a couple of times to adjust to the lighting and gasped. I stared at my reflection; my skin was completely white and my hair had turned black.

"Whoa," Liu said.

"Oh Jeffery, it's not so bad," my mom said and put her hand on my shoulder.

"What are you talking about? It's perfect I love it!" I grabbed Naomi's hand and placed it on my cheek. "You like it too right?" She ran a finger down my cheek.

"No, I don't like it," she said with a serious look on her face.

"What, why?" I frowned. She looked at me.

"I don't like it, I love it." She smiled widely and kissed me. I kissed her back.

"Eww, you two are gross!" Liu said. I backed off first.

"Alright I'll get your mom to fill out some paperwork and then you're free to go," the nurse said and left with my mom.

"I can't believe everything is still intact," Naomi said while playing with my hair.

"Yeah, I'm surprised as well." She rubbed my arm and I blushed.

"Jeff, your skin feels a little like leather," she said.

"I can't really tell honestly," I said.

"You two are making me sick," Liu said and stuck out his tongue.

"Then leave if this makes you feel sick." I kissed Naomi just to make Liu feel uncomfortable.

"Seriously Jeff that's gross!" Liu said and ran out of the room.

"Oh, I brought you some clothes," she said and pulled away from me to grab a bag that was on the floor and handed it to me. I opened it and pulled out a white hoodie and black dress pants.

"I thought this stuff burned," I said a little confused.

"Oh it did. I just went out and bought you some new stuff." Naomi smiled at me.

"Well thanks." I went into the bathroom and changed. I walked out of the bathroom.

"Come on guys! Mom is done with the paperwork, let's go home," Liu said.

I walked out of the room and followed Liu with Naomi trailing behind us.

Naomi's Perspective

I was glad Jeff was ok, but something seemed a little off about him. I just didn't know what. I walked beside him and took his hand. He looked at me and he blushed.

"Oh, you should know that Keith was caught but Troy got away," I said.

"How can you lose a fat kid?" He sighed.

"I was wondering the same thing." I looked down as we walked back to the car. I looked at my phone clock it was 9:30 pm. I yawned a little.

"Are you tired?" He asked and looked at me.

"Yeah, I've been up the past three nights worrying about you," I smiled weakly.

"You didn't have to do that you know," he said.

"Yeah, I know. I was just really worried and when I worry I don't sleep."

We walked into the large underground parking lot. My vision clouded over and I got light headed. I let go of Jeff's hand and started to lag a little behind. I tried to keep walking but it felt like my legs wouldn't move. I started to breath heavily. I fell to the ground, vomited a little blood and passed out. I heard voices, but I couldn't make out what they were saying.

I woke up in my room with a cold rag over my head. It looked like it was morning. I coughed.

"Oh, you're awake." My mom came in and took the rag off my head and stuck a thermometer in my mouth.

"You fainted in the hospital parking lot and Jeff's mom brought you home." She took the thermometer out of my mouth and looked at it. "It's 99.9 degrees, you still have a little bit of a temperature, but that doesn't mean you can't have visitors." She left the room.

"I don't feel like seeing anyone." I tucked my head under the covers.

"Not even me?" I looked over the covers to see Jeff in the doorway. I rolled over.

"Can I come in?" he asked.

"Sure I guess." He came in and sat on the edge of my bed.

"Brought you something you might like," he said.

"What is it?"

He handed me a gold box with a black ribbon. I shook it.

"Can I open it?" I asked and he nodded.

I opened it to see different kinds of chocolates. My eyes grew big. "Where did you get this?" I grabbed a chocolate.

"I got it from a homeless man across the street," he said.

I put the chocolate down.

"I'm joking, I bought it." I picked it back up and popped it in my mouth.

"You didn't have to get me anything you know," I said and set the box on my bedside table.

"Yeah, I know, but you bought me clothes so I bought you chocolate."

I blew some hair out of my face and sat up.

"I guess I should have slept those three days instead of staying awake the whole time," I said.

"Yeah, that would have been best." He laughed a little.

"I don't want to be here all day, I want to do something!"

I yelled into my pillow. My mom came in.

"You can get out of bed; just don't run around or stuff." She left.

I hopped out of bed, grabbed some clothes and ran into the bathroom to change. I walked out and headed downstairs into the living room and sat at the piano. Jeff came down and stood behind me.

"You play the piano?" he asked.

"Yeah, I used to take lessons when I was really little."
I picked up a piece of sheet music and put it on the
stand and began playing. I played *Vector to the
Heavens* from the game *Kingdom Hearts 358/2 Days*. I
played and hummed along to it. I stopped and let the
piano ring for a moment.

"Wow that's amazing." I looked at Jeff's face and saw
he was really stunned. "Could you play something
else?" he asked.

"Of course I can." I chose to play *Kingdom Hearts
Sanctuary*. I played and started singing without
knowing it. I hit the last note and held it for as long
as I could. I let the piano ring once again. I leaned
back in the chair.

"Wow!" Jeff said. "I honestly have no words to
describe how amazing that was."

"I'm not that good," I said and put the sheet music
away.

"You are beyond good: you're amazing!"

I laughed a little. "Thanks." I got up.

"Come to think of it I taught myself something on the
piano once," Jeff said and took my place at the piano.
"I'll see if I can try and remember it." He pressed
some of the keys. "If you know it you can sing to it."
He smiled at me.

"Ok I'll try."

He began playing. I recognized the song instantly; it
was *Sweet Dreams Are Made of These*. I knew it but I
got a weird feeling when I began singing it. I sang
along with the piano until I noticed Jeff had started
singing along with me. Things became jumbled in my

mind, visions of creepy things that made no sense to me whatsoever. My whole body began to feel weird. The song ended and I quickly sat down.

"You ok?" Jeff got up and kneeled in front of me. I looked into his eyes.

"Yeah, I'm just out of breath. I don't really sing that often."

"This may sound like and odd question, but do you dance?" he asked me.

"I dance when no one is around, like when I'm left home alone. I dance to music on my computer that I hook up to some speakers so I can hear it throughout the house."

He laughed.

"Yeah, I know." I rolled my eyes.

He stood up and held his hand out to me and I took it.

"Want to dance with me?"

My face reddened. "Like right now?"

He nodded.

"I guess that's fine."

He pulled a white box out of his pocket and plugged it into his phone and pressed a button. I gasped a little and realized the song was *Fallen Angel*.

'It's like my imagination realm all over again.'

Jeff's Perspective

I flipped the music on. I wasn't one for love music and all, but it was the only song I had that was danceable. I took her hand and placed my other hand on her waist. She put her other hand on my back and I moved slowly and she followed. We stopped dancing and the music kept playing. She looked at me confused until I placed my lips to hers. She placed her head on my shoulder. We stood there for what seemed like forever.

"Jeff?" she said.

"Yes, Naomi?"

"You made one of my imaginations come true." I brushed hair out of my face.

"I'm glad I could make you happy."

My phone buzzed and I let her hand go and looked at it.

"I have to go back home." I put my phone and speaker in my pocket.

"I'll go with you." She said and took my hand.

"If you want to that's fine with me," I said and gripped her hand tightly.

"You might want to tell your mom before you go," I said.

"Oh right." She ran off and I waited by the front door. She came back. "Ok, I'm ready now." She opened the door and we walked outside. I held her hand.

"Hey, you two idiots almost cost me my life!" I heard someone yell behind us. I turned around and saw Troy standing a few feet away from us he was holding a gun.

"This won't turn out so well," I said.

"Oh, it will turn out well for me, but not for you guys," he said.

"Hey, look an ice cream truck!" He looked behind him and I took off dragging Naomi behind me.

"Hey, I don't see no ice cream truck," Keith said and turned around, but we were gone.

I laughed.

"That's fat guys for you," I said and walked up my driveway. I looked behind me.

"What's wrong?"

"I have to walk back that way: I could get killed!" She trembled. I froze and images flashed in my mind of blood everywhere and her dead body.

"You can stay here for a while until he leaves." We walked inside.

"JEFF YOU'RE BACK!" Liu yelled when I came in.

"Nice to see you to Liu," I said.

Liu went back to watching his show on the couch. I walked into the kitchen and grabbed a bottle of water and walked back in the room to find Naomi standing by the window looking outside. I stood next to her.

"There's a storm coming in," she said.

"I hate storms," Liu said and tossed a pillow in the air.

"How can you tell?" I asked looking at the sky.

"See those dark gray clouds rolling in fast? Those are storm clouds," she said.

I poked a hole in the top of the water bottle.

"Watch this," I said. I walked behind Liu and squirted the water down his shirt.

"Ah! That's freezing!" He fell off the couch. I laughed. I looked over at Naomi who was trying to hold her laugh in.

"That's not funny, Jeff." Liu threw a pillow at me but he missed.

"You missed me by a mile," I said.

"What if I wasn't trying to hit you?" He gave me that smug look of his.

"If you were trying to hit me, it didn't work," Naomi said and threw the pillow back at him whacking him in the face. Liu looked dazed for a minute.

"Nice throw Nao," he said.

"Wait you caught that?" I asked confused.

"I have good reflexes." I stood there for a second.

"Are you positive you have good reflexes?" I asked and picked up another pillow.

"Yeah, I'm positive," she said and turned away from me. I threw the pillow and hit her in the back of the head making her head snap forward and hit the window.

"Jeez man, you didn't have to throw the pillow so hard," Liu said and laughed.

She stumbled and hit the floor.

"Ouch, that really hurt." She held her head.

"Oops, I honestly didn't mean to throw it that hard, maybe I should have waited till you turned around," I said.

"Hey, at least I'm not bleeding this time," she said.

"Yeah, your head might hurt for a while though," Liu said.

She got up and looked out the window again.

"I think I'm safe to go." She opened the door. "See you later." She walked out and down the street and disappeared around the corner. It began to rain hard.

"She was right," I said and then I heard it. A gun shot rang throughout the neighborhood.

"What in the world was that?" Liu peeked over the couch.

I grabbed the biggest knife I could find in the knife drawer and ran outside in the rain. I ran down the street and round the corner and saw Keith in Naomi's front yard.

"Well, what do we have here, another one come for killing I presume." Keith pointed the gun at me.

"No way you can dodge a bullet pipsqueak," he said.

"I'm feeling lucky today," I said.

He shot the gun, but nothing came out, only a puff of smoke. Keith dropped the gun and ran.

"Not so fast!" I threw the knife as hard as I could and it lodged itself into his head. I ran into the yard and knelt in the grass. Naomi's mom came running out.

"I heard a gunshot and called the police and an ambulance," she said. She looked down and cried out. "Oh please not my little girl!" The ambulance pulled up and two medics jumped out of the back and put Naomi on a stretcher.

"Do you two need a ride to the hospital?" the woman asked.

I nodded and hopped in the back of the ambulance as the woman helped Naomi's mom in the back. I sat there in silence. As soon as we got to the hospital I jumped out and they rolled her away to an emergency surgery room. Her mom sat in a chair outside the room while I paced back and forth.

I got a text from Liu. *'Where are you?'*

I texted him back. *'At the hospital there's been an accident.'* I sent the message and instantly got a reply back.

'Mom and I are on our way now.' I paced some more. Liu ran in through the double doors and crashed into me.

"Ouch." I rubbed my head.

"Sorry Jeff," Liu said and helped me up.

"How's she doing?" my mom asked.

"That's just it; I haven't heard anything." I frowned and paced more.

"If you keep pacing like that you'll wear a hole in the floor," Liu said.

I stopped walking and sat down. The door to the surgery room opened and a doctor came out of it. I looked up as he talked to Naomi's mom. I sneaked away and looked into the surgery room.

"It's empty." I held back tears. I walked back out and sat down.

"What's wrong with you Jeff? You should be happy," Liu said.

"Why should I be happy?" I asked super confused.

"You didn't hear the news, did you?" he asked. I shook my head.

"They got the bullets out; it missed her heart and brain by a millimeter," he said. I breathed a sigh of relief.

"If you want to go see her she's in the first room down the hall," my mom said.

I walked down the hall and looked into the room. She was sitting up in the bed with this bored look on her face. She also had a bandage that wrapped itself around her eye and around her head.

"Hey." I walked into the room and her face lit up. "Hi."

"How are you feeling?" I asked.

"Well, my chest and head hurt really badly." She frowned.

"Liu told me the bullet missed your heart and brain by a millimeter," I said.

"I guess I'm just lucky like you." She smiled a little. I sat down on the edge of the bed.

"I have food for the patient." Liu poked his head in.

"What kind of food?" she asked.

"Well, you have a chicken quesadilla, two tacos, and two cinnamon twist looking things," Liu said peering in the bag.

I got up and took the bag.

"Thanks little brother." I handed her the bag.

"I guess my mom got enough food for the two of us." She said.

She took the food out of the bag and handed me my portion of stuff. I ate and looked in the mirror the room.

"Do I look beautiful to you?" I asked without thinking.

"What?" she asked.

"I said do I look beautiful to you, I mean the way I look now." I looked into her eyes.

"Yes you do."

I stared deeper into her eyes.

"Good, you aren't lying to me." I smiled widely.

Chapter 6

NAOMI'S PERSPECTIVE

'Why did he ask me if I thought he was beautiful?
Something must have happened to him when he was in
that fight with Randy: something snapped,' I thought.
I got up off the bed and walked around.
"I'm so bored! I don't like being cooped up in a place
for a long time." I turned back around.
"Hey, get up." I laughed at Jeff who was lying on the
bed with my heart monitor acting dead.
"I can't move, I'm dead," he said.
"Oh well excuse me. I thought dead people didn't
talk." I jumped on the bed knocking him off. I put the
heart monitor on and the beeping was fast, then it
slowed down.
"I guess I can't get too worked up, huh?"
Jeff hopped up off the ground.
"I guess not," he said and sat back down. He looked
at me and I looked into his eyes. They were still
crystal blue.
"Jeff honey, it's time to go. Oh and Naomi, you are
being released later tonight." His mom walked out.
"Alright, thank you."
Jeff kissed my check and walked out of the room.

JEFF'S PERSPECTIVE

I walked out of the room and walked with my mom and brother to the car.

I heard a voice inside my head. *'Hey, Jeff did you like killing Randy and Keith?'*

I mumbled, "Yeah, I liked it a lot."

'You also think you're beautiful right?'

I nodded and whispered like I was talking to someone. "I do think that, but every time I close my eyes I can't see myself."

'Then do something about it,' the voice said. I nodded. We drove home and I walked upstairs and flopped on the bed. It was getting late I fell asleep and woke up in the middle of the night.

"The voice was right; I can't see myself when I sleep."

I snuck downstairs and rummaged around the kitchen and took out a knife and lighter. I snuck back upstairs and shut the bathroom door. I lit the lighter and burned my eyelids off. I cried.

I took the knife and slid it into my mouth, cutting my cheeks from ear to ear in a permanent smile. Blood dripped down on to the sink.

I heard the door open and I heard someone gasp. I turned around and saw my mom standing there.

"Hello mommy," I said.

"Jeffery, what did you do?" She backed up.

"I couldn't see how beautiful I was so I burned my eyelids off and I cut a permanent smile into my cheeks so now I can be happy all the time."
I smiled some. "Tell me mommy, am I beautiful?" I asked hopefully.
"Yes you are dear let me get your father so he can see how beautiful you are too."
She ran out of the room and back to their room.
"Honey, get up and get your gun! Jeff is…" She stopped as I opened the door.
"Mommy you lied." I walked in. "YOU LIED TO ME!" I held the knife and slit open her neck and stabbed my father.

LIU'S PERSPECTIVE

I was having trouble sleeping. I thought I heard a yell but I must be still half asleep. I heard a creaking outside my door and it opened slowly.
I screamed!
"Shhh Liu, it's only me," Jeff said.
He walked over to my bed side and held my throat.
"Shhh, just go to sleep Liu," he said.
I felt something sharp go into my chest. I coughed up blood. I slipped away into nothingness.

JEFF'S PERSPECTIVE

I looked at the blood covered knife.

"Now where shall I go next?"

I walked down the street in the pouring rain and down to the big white house. Something in the back of my mind nagged me to not go. I ignored it and walked up to the house and tried the front door handle.

"It's locked."

I stuck my knife in the crack and pried open the door. I stepped inside. I heard a quiet piano playing. I walked toward the sound of the piano and stepped into the room.

"Hello there Jeff, how are you this fine rainy night?" Naomi turned around.

"Aren't you scared of me?" I asked.

She shook her head. "Of course I'm not scared of you; why would I be?"

She walked over to me. I backed away.

"Don't worry, I won't kill you. I'd never want to do that." She smiled at me. She blew hair out of her face and I noticed that there was a cut along both of her eyes and a heart cut into her cheek.

"You're like me now," I said.

"I heard a voice talk to me; it said kill, so I killed," she said.

"What did you kill?" I asked.

She took my hand and led me to a room. I looked and saw two figures on the bed.

"You killed your parents like I did?" I said.
She nodded. "It was so fun; I want to kill more people!" She laughed.
"We can go kill as many as we want!" I said.
"I want to kill everyone who made my life miserable," she said.
I nodded in agreement.
She walked away and came back in a gray hoodie. She carried a knife.
"Let's go! Like I said before, I don't like being any place for too long."
I took her hand and we walked through the streets to fulfill the dream of becoming the best killers ever.

NEWS REPORT

"This just in: we have news that two teens, Jeffery and Naomi, have gone missing from the same neighborhood," the reporter said. "We have police on the scene now and the houses are empty except for the dead family of these teens." We are not sure what has happened to them, but people have been saying that there have been deaths happening throughout their neighborhood every night. One boy was lucky enough to survive one of these attacks."
The screen switches to a boy about ten years old.
"So tell us, can you describe these two killers for us?" the woman asked.

"Yes, um, there was a teenage boy and girl about the same age. The boy had black hair and black circles around his eyes and a permanent smile cut into his face. Oh, he also had a white hoodie on. The girl had two cuts on her eyes and a heart shaped cut on her cheek. She had a gray hoodie on." The little boy shivered.

"Anything else you want to tell us?" the lady asked.

"Yes, the boy told me to go to sleep before he stabbed me. My dad came in with his gun at the last minute, but the boy threw his knife and it went into his shoulder. He was killed by the teenage girl. She came out of nowhere! I thought it was just the boy; I didn't have time to warn my dad!" He cried a little.

"You heard it here everyone," the lady said.

"They are after me!" the boy said. "The girl said I couldn't escape; she said they would find me and kill me." He shook.

The door to the news room opened.

"Hey you two can't be in here we are shooting the latest story!" The lady stood up. A boy and a girl stood in the doorway.

"Oh and what story would that be?" the girl asked.

"It's about these two killers and this young boy here was telling us about them."

The boy in the white hoodie laughed. "Sounds interesting."

The little boy screamed.

"WE HAVE TO GET OUT OF HERE NOW! CAN'T YOU SEE THESE ARE THE TWO KILLERS I WAS TALKING ABOUT!"

The lady looked closely at the two hooded figures. "I never show my face on public news," the girl said. She walked around the camera and jumped on the table in front of the little boy.

"Don't be scared sweetie, all you need is pain." The knife was thrust into the boy's neck and heart. His blood spattered all over the place and over the camera. She cut a small heart into his cheek. There was the thud of the boy's body on the ground. The hooded boy walked around the camera and stood in front of the news reporter. She gasped at the sight of his face.

"Shhh, go to sleep." The boy in the white hoodie slit the woman's neck, making blood go everywhere. Then he stabbed her in the chest and cut a smile into her face. The girl moved in front of the camera, but you could barely make out what she looked like.

"Don't worry everyone, we'll be coming for you next and I'll make sure to carve a heart in your cheek to show that you were loved." She moved aside and the boy took her place.

"For all of you who are seeing this right now, we'll find you too so you needn't feel left out. And don't worry, I'll cut a smile into your face and make you beautiful just like me."

The camera shut off and everything is quiet.

EPILOUGE

The girl and boy have moved on and traveled to a
new place to kill.

They enter some woods and come across a mansion
at the end of the woods. There is a tall man with long
arms and legs. He is so tall that he blends in well
with the trees.

The two walk over to him.

"Welcome to the mansion of killers, we have been
awaiting your arrival Jeff and Naomi."

The two killers look at each other and entered the
house where they were met by a group of teens, a
little girl, and a dog. A boy with a mask covering his
mouth walked over.

"I'm T-Toby," the boy said twitching.

"I'm Sally, wanna play with me?" the little girl asked.
The dog barked and gave a huge smile.

"I'm Masky and that's Smile dog," a boy with a white
mask said.

"I'm Hoody," the boy in an orange hood waved to
the new members of the family. A boy that looked
like Link from *The Legend of Zelda* games came over,
but he had brown hair and blood was dripping from
his eyes.

"My name is Ben," he said.

"I'm Eyeless Jack but call me E.J." a boy with a blue
mask that covered his eyes said.

"And I am Slenderman. There are other killers but they are followers of Zalgo and sometimes they may want to fight you," the tall man in the suit said.

"So we've met everyone, now what?" Jeff asked.

42973948R00044

Made in the USA
Lexington, KY
22 June 2019